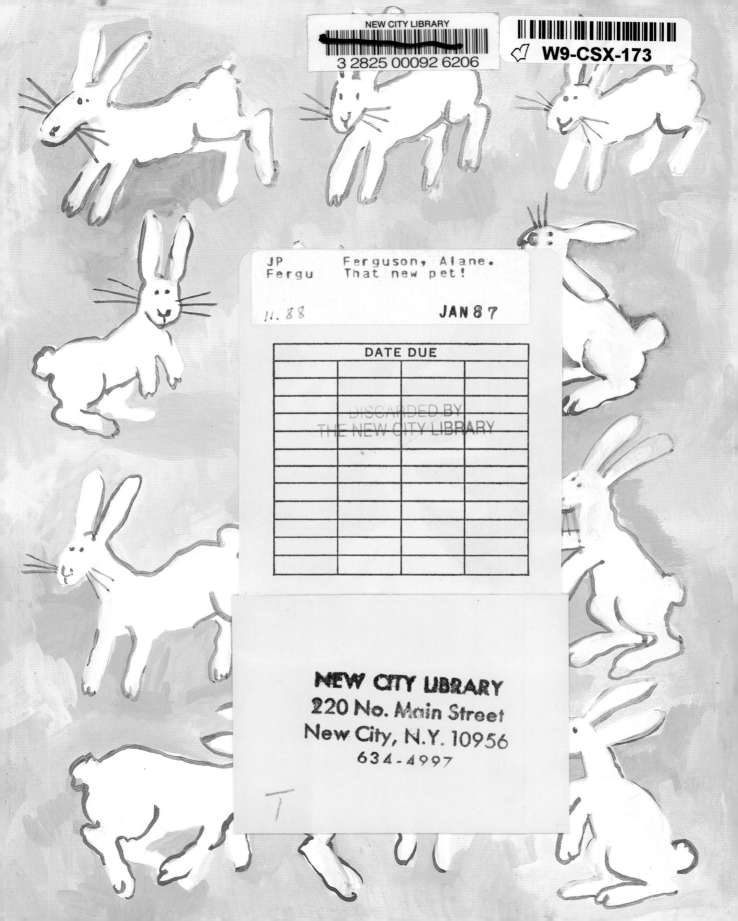

Alane Ferguson
THAT NEW PET!

Pictures by
Catherine Stock

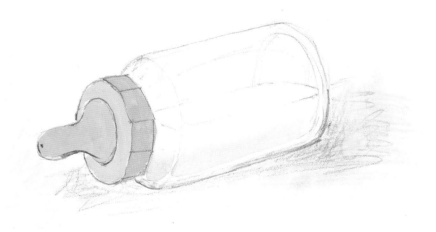

LOTHROP, LEE & SHEPARD BOOKS
NEW YORK

1 2 3 4 5 6 7 8 9 10

Library of Congress Cataloging in Publication Data
Ferguson, Alane.   That new pet!
   Summary: The household animals are puzzled by the tailless, featherless, noisy, messy new pet their
owners bring home—it's a baby. [1. Babies—Fiction. 2. Animals—Fiction] I. Stock, Catherine, ill.
II. Title. PZ7.F3547Th 1986 [E] 85-23911
ISBN 0-688-05515-X
ISBN 0-688-05516-8 (lib. bdg.)

To my teacher,
my inspiration,
my mother
–A. F.

For Tanya and Liesl
and their new pets
–C. S.

*O*ur house was exactly the right size for all of us. There was Crackers, the parrot; Bones, the springer spaniel; and of course, me.

I'm Siam, the Siamese cat.

Our owners, Joanie and Teddy, lived with us too. Everything was just the way it was supposed to be.

That's why we were puzzled when Joanie and Teddy came home holding a brand-new pet.

Crackers was the first one to introduce himself. He perched on Teddy's shoulder, tilted his head, and blinked one eye. "Hello, there," he squawked. "Glad to have you aboard."

"Crackers, be quiet!" Teddy whispered. "You'll wake her up."

Crackers stared a long time, then ruffled his feathers and flew down to me. "Siam," he said, "this is not an ordinary bird. It doesn't have any feathers—not one. And guess what else."

"No beak?" I suggested.

"That's right. And it doesn't have wings, either. You'd better take a look."

Before I had a chance, Bones bounded over, wiggling his silly tail.

"Down, Bones. Down!" Joanie said. "Naughty doggie!"

Bones sadly sniffed a welcome and padded back to me. "Siam," he said, "this is not an ordinary dog. It doesn't have any teeth. And guess what else."

"No tail?" I ventured.

"That's right. It certainly is the darnedest thing. You'd better take a look."

When I jumped beside the new pet on Joanie's lap, Teddy scooped me up and dumped me hard on the kitchen floor.

"Scram," he said.

I didn't want them to know how much their rudeness bothered me. So I rolled over, yawned, and *strrretched* myself as far as I could reach.

Then I sauntered into the living room.

Bones and Crackers came, too.

"Siam," Bones asked, "do you think they'll keep it? It can't even walk!"

"It can't fly," Crackers added, "and it can't feed itself from a dish."

"I noticed it isn't housebroken," Bones said. "Do you think they got it from the pound?"

"Friends," I said, "I've seen this type of pet before. It's called a *baby*. And when a baby comes—EVERYTHING CHANGES!"

My announcement was greeted with stunned silence.

After a while Bones moaned, "Why would Joanie and Teddy do a thing like that? Weren't we enough to keep them happy?"

"They act as if we're in the way," Crackers complained. "What are we going to do?"

"Friends," I answered, "I've heard stories about these baby-pets. They wake up and scream and need diapers changed, at all hours of the day and night."

"Don't the owners put them outside?" Bones asked.

"They make horrible gooey messes and drip unspeakable things when they eat," I said.

"Can't the owners keep them in a cage?" Crackers asked.

I said, "It is my opinion that we will have to out-charm this new pet. If we're all very good, Joanie and Teddy will see that *we* don't cause problems. *We* don't make messes. They'll see that things were better the way they were before. *Sssssssso*," I hissed, "they'll decide to take the baby back where it came from."

For the next few weeks we were all on excellent behavior. Crackers stopped his 6 A.M. squally-squawks and quit drizzling birdseed on the floor. Bones no longer buried chew toys in Joanie and Teddy's bed, and he drank from his water dish instead of the toilet. Of course, I was already extremely well mannered, but to be even better, I forced myself to eat that horrid cat food they buy for me.

But no matter what we tried, Joanie and Teddy hardly paid attention to us. And worst of all, the new pet was still there.

We decided to meet again.

Bones drooped his head on his paws. His nose began to quiver. "I nuzzled Teddy's feet for five minutes, but he wouldn't scratch my head," he said. "He was too busy making faces at the baby."

Crackers puffed himself into a big bright ball. He began to hop from foot to foot. "I waited until ten o'clock for Joanie to change my birdseed. But she's always feeding that— that—"

"That good-for-nothing pet," I spat. "Friends, we've tried being nice to get attention. It didn't work. *Sssssso*...let us try being AWFUL!"

For the next few weeks the three of us were
unspeakably bad. I won't go into much detail.

Suffice it to say, at one point I found myself airborne. Teddy sent me sailing through the back door, and I landed none too gently on the porch.

I looked to the left. There stood Crackers, a drooping rainbow.

I looked to the right. Bone's eyes blinked forlornly. "Banished, we three," he sniffed. "Outcasts. Fugitives. Criminals." He draped his sad mooshy mouth across his paws, waiting for us to be called back inside.

Hours later, we were still on the porch. Teddy had gone shopping, and Joanie was in the basement doing the wash. She couldn't hear the baby crying.

It began to wail. "*A-la-a-la-a!*"

"Oh, my heavens," Bones said.

Then it began to scream. "*Yaaaeee!*"

"Great balls of fire!" Crackers squawked. "We have to do something."

Bones pushed himself through the doggie door, and Crackers followed him into the house. I stayed outside, alone with my dignity.

Slowly the baby's cries grew softer.

And softer.

Then they stopped.

My curiosity got the best of me. "Dignity be hanged," I said, pushing through the doggie door.

I found an exhausted Crackers next to the baby's cradle. He looked like the end of a feather duster.

"Siam, guess what," he said. "The baby kicked my beak and pulled out my tail feathers, but I got her to stop crying."

"She yanked my ears and tweaked my nose,"
Bones added. "But I made her smile."

I leaped onto the cradle's headboard and looked down. The baby bent back her head and looked up at me.

Slowly I leaned farther.

And farther.

Our noses touched. I wiggled my whiskers.

I heard a sudden sound bubbing up from that troublesome pet. It started as a gurgle and ended as a giggly squeal. She laughed. For me!

Crackers had made her stop crying. Bones had made her smile. But only I had made her laugh out loud. That good-for-nothing pet was good for me, Siam, the Siamese cat.

Now, once again our house is exactly the right size for all of us: for Joanie and Teddy, Bones and Crackers, and me and the baby, too. I persuaded Bones and Crackers to keep her after all.